EXPRESSIONS FROM THE HEART

(An anthology containing poems by women writers around the world)

Edited & Compiled By
Ishita Ganguly

Published by InkQuills Publishing House
www.inkquills.in

First Edition 2022

ISBN: 978-93-90567-30-0

DISCLAIMER

The published write-ups are the original contents of the co-authors and compiler had done her best to edit and make it plagiarism free.

The characters may be fictitious or based on real events but they are not meant to hurt anyone's feeling nor portray anything against any caste or system.

In case of any plagiarized write-up the co-author is solely responsible for it, Compiler or Publisher would not be responsible for it.

Ishita Ganguly

"Look, I am not rich but I had a gem,
I lost him in the blink of an eye —
My best friend, my first teacher, my father.
There are two worlds for me now —
In one it was full of light where I was with my father
And in this one, it's pitch dark.
In this one, I am fatherless and alone."

- Ishita Ganguly

Dedicated to

My father, Late Sri Benu Ganguly

A Letter Of Thanks From The Editor

I started collecting pieces from woman Poets around the world at the start of 2021. The year we all have wished and prayed would free the world from the pandemic. But it didn't. I got absorbed in my personal and professional commitments and this anthology project got delayed.

Then at the beginning of 2022, when I have worked halfway on this book, my father fell ill and was hospitalized. He was struggling somewhere between life and death and I was hoping and praying for his recovery. But he closed his life chapter and left us on 7th February. My biggest cheerleader, my most avid reader, my father will not read this book but I know I have finally been able to complete this grand project because of his blessings. I have been able to record the works of 40 women Poets from 15 countries in the very book you are holding now! If this is not a blessing, what is? My father believed that work must be carried on. So, I am doing my work. I am writing every single day. I have also written a piece the day he passed away. I live through my writing and my father lives through me.

I congratulate each of the writers whose poem has been selected in this anthology. Some of you are professional writers, some of you are amateurs but always remember we all have come together because of our common love for writing, for creating something new, to tell a poem to the world.

Life is larger than Poetry. But Poetry lives longer than life. Or so I believe.

I wanted to compile an all-women anthology because I think women writers are hugely under-represented in most countries.

Dear Poetess, this is your platform to express your voice. You are not only a woman but you are a Poet, and you have goddess-like power in creating something new out of thin air, in creating a poem that you can proudly share with the world!

Guru kripa hi kevalam

Love and light,
Ishita Ganguly
Author & Freelance Writer
Author of *Stories from the City called Kolkata*
Instagram: *@iamauthorishita*
Website: *www.ishitaganguly.com*

CONTENTS

Co-Authors From Incredible India:

Ishita Ganguly

(Kolkata, India)

The Sleeping River

The sleeping river emerges
from the depth of my heart,
passing the crevices and safely reaching out to the world.
People long lost resurface
in my dreams
and flow with the river
that dried up ages ago
in a forgotten summer.
Faces reappear,
so do the memories.
I drown in the river
in my dream.
I ask for help
seeing the known faces
standing absently on the shore
looking at me
like I am a stranger to them.
I beg for forgiveness,
they don't look at me –
their stony faces don't reflect any mercy.
'But I have forgiven you all, won't you forgive me?' I ask.
They don't blink or look at me
while I keep drowning in the river.
Some nights I die in the dream,
some nights I float on the surface of the sleeping river.

[The Sleeping River was first published in The Monograph magazine, November 2021 issue]

About the Poet:

Ishita Ganguly is a published author, Poet, freelance writer, and editor from India. She writes in both English and Bangla. Writing is her passion, obsession and now her full-time profession. She is the author of the book, "Stories from the City called Kolkata". Her articles have been published in prestigious Indian newspapers like The Times of India and The Hindu. Over 100 articles and poems written by her have been published in several renowned international magazines and websites. Her writing courses are available on Udemy, the world's number 1 learning platform. She has been interviewed by youth magazines and featured in podcasts.

She is a co-author of three international anthologies – "Ardour", "Pivot and Pause" and "What if Love Happens Again?"

Ishita is a double master's degree holder, a corporate professional turned educator turned full-time writer. She is a book lover who believes words have immense power and writers can make a huge impact in the world! She desires to leave the world better than she found it through her contributions as a writer and as a responsible global citizen.

You can follow Ishita on Instagram & Twitter **@iamauthorishita**, on LinkedIn, YouTube and Quora -> **Ishita Ganguly** and Website: **www.ishitaganguly.com**

Cristina Munoz

(Woodend, Australia)

Grateful

Caught in grief's grip
I find myself grateful
For craving the calm
Of your glowing skin
Which sets so gently
Like a golden sunset
Gorgeous against my own
Before sinking slowly
Beneath a blue horizon
Soothing my hot sorrow
With such cooling
Winter light

About the Poet:

Cristina Munoz (or Cris) is a Spanish/Australian soft butch (L)GBTQ+ mainly lyrical published Poet living in Australia currently working on her first manuscript. She is also a co-writer of the single 'Going Home' by an international indie band, Tiny Fighter. You can follow Cris on Twitter & Instagram Handle: @cristinamunoz8

Karen E Fraser

(Melbourne, Australia)

We Are Everyday Remarkable

we are e v e r y - d a y - r e m a r k a b l e
women e m e r g i n g united
endless grace, living in place
distant lands - login close
flying friendship flags
fabric of hope
r e s i l e n t
brilliant
notes
..
f u l l
souls ripe
g a t h e r i n g
welcome in w o r d s
fruit from lives lived well
voices w r i t i n g bell-clear
home-truth hearts growing strong
- a la c e w o r k of d i v i n i t y -
each breathtaking expression is l o v e

About the Poet:
Karen E Fraser is a published Poet/writer with degrees in Professional and Creative Writing and Anthropology. She utilizes the storytelling of belonging and dignity to illuminate truth, social justice, and Oneness.
Instagram Handle: @be_nourished

Setraj Jahan

(Dhaka, Bangladesh)

Just Let The Nights Be Mine

I will give you my days
just let the nights be mine,

I want some lone time
to explore all glorious signs,

This vast world
in which countless riddles whine,

Tales of Phoenix and Unicorn
make the stars of my eyes shine,

The night is the only way
for those bitter truths to decline,

I hope, I hope again
someday I will be fine,

I will give you my days —
just let the nights be mine.

About the Poet:

Setraj Jahan is a freelance content writer, Poetry lover, and artist. Her poems and photography have been published in international magazines.
Instagram Handle: @setrajstories

Courtney Tudman

(Niagara Falls, Canada)

Stay With Me

I had a dream
You dressed all in black
Sweeping a concrete floor
With a hard bristle broom

I flew into the room
And flopped on a single bed
Much like the one
We shared in college

You laughed, as you often did at me
Your strong chin resting
Atop the smoothed out
Wood handle

That smile, oh, that smile
The one that captured my breath
The first time we collided
In a dimly lit corridor

It was in that instant
When we decided
Some souls are
Destined to meet

I had a dream
And as you turned your body
To push dust into the far
Corner of the room

I reached out and cried
"Please, don't go!"

For I knew that if I lost this dream
I would lose you too

I awoke
A forever too soon
A lifetime too short
Never to be seen again

About the Poet:
Courtney Tudman has been an avid reader, writer, and learner from a young age. She loves raising her son and surrounding herself with friends and family. Courtney works in the social services sector where she enjoys helping others achieve their best quality of life.
Instagram Handle: @courtneytudman.writes

Loveleen Kaur

(Calgary, Canada)

She Is A Warrior

She is bleeding heavily
And is expected to do her duty fully.
Her body is aching and breaking,
But she needs to pretend like nothing's happening.
She is consciously checking her back for the stain
While constantly suffering from unbearable pain.
"The pads should be kept out of sight", she is being told.
The idea of freely discussing menstruation is always wrong.
She is experiencing a natural flow,
But, shh, people shouldn't get to know!
Despite the fact that it's something
that will support life and will help a zygote to grow.
Her periods are not an embarrassing matter.
She is a daughter, a wife, a mother, and a warrior.
She keeps fighting and surviving like a wounded soldier.
Remember, she has reasons enough to be proud just to be her.

About the Poet:

Loveleen Kaur is a writer by passion. She is an international student based in Canada. She thinks her inner voice is taking the form of words to give courage and determination to her as well as others.

Susan Koppersmith

(Vancouver BC, Canada)

Parts Of Her Emerging

My right calf
Scooped out
By an oncologist 40 years ago
Its absence
Covered always now
With dark cloth

This mark of disgrace
A stigma
Not of my making
A badge of honor
For a
Reluctant
Warrior

At the louvre
The Venus de milo
Charms her admirers
With imagined arms
The apple
In her left hand
Wholly there

I hardly
Can speak
Of my battle
But
I can speak for Venus
That orb of light

Shining round her
And the way people
Love her bold eyes
And
Keep rediscovering
Parts of her
Emerging
From what's
Missing

About the Poet:
Susan Koppersmith is a Poet living in Vancouver, Canada. She has had poems published in online journals and enjoys, when it is her turn, to lead her writing group.

Tanja Ajtic
(Vancouver, Canada)

Why

Why are you running when I'm not looking for you in the first place?
Who are you hiding from?
Why are you leaving when I'm not waiting for you?
You did it long ago.
Why are you angry when I forgave you all?
Because you cannot do it to me!
Why don't you look at me when I see you?
In everything.
Why are you scared I don't understand?
When I know you're free and yours.
Why are you scared I'm going to call you?
Who to call Invisible?
Maybe your shadow?
Why are you disappearing?
However, I am not anywhere.
I'm nowhere.
Why to lie?

About the Poet:
Tanja Ajtic is a freelance artist from Serbia who now lives in Canada. She is a Poet, writer, and graphic artist. Her poems have been published in ninety collections, anthologies, and magazines. Her poems have been published in seven languages. She has published a book of Poetry "Contours of Love".

Diana Wiese

(Bensheim, Germany)

August Night Sky

Falling stars burn up
On their way down from the sky.
Hold on, rushing Beauty, to watch
These brief moments of joy,
Sweet fragments of time.

They remind us
There is no glory
In being busy;
Life is not a race—
We do not know
Where and what the aim is
Nor who and what we run against.

We must set our own pace,
Extend our silent glow,
And applaud ourselves—
Much longer than it takes
For a falling star to hit the ground.

About the Poet:
Diana Wiese is a writer at heart, translator, and mother who left the corporate world after her son was born. Writing is her way of paying attention. Her writings are inspired by the mundane as well as the peculiar. She focuses on storytelling through prose-poems and micro-memoir. Diana holds an M.A. in American Studies and has previously been published in the anthologies "Pivot and Pause" and "365 Days of Covid".
Instagram Handle: @wiesentau

Mirjam Mahler

(Ulm, Germany)

On The Other Side

On an old train
Going really fast
Swallowed by a tunnel
The world goes dark
Sounds are muffled
Time stops
On the other side
The world is bright
Colors shine
I was here all along
I will be here
Next time

About the Poet:
Mirjam Mahler writes poems and stories and finds great joy in reading the words from others and in helping others find their words. She was born in Germany, raised in Spain, went to university in the US and is now living in the south of Germany with her husband, two teenage sons and an adopted cat. She offers workshop to introduce women to the short form Poetry she loves.
Instagram Handle: @mirjamwrites

Tali Cohen Shabtai

(Jerusalem, Israel)

Sunset Before Sunrise?

'The sunset is preparation for the strengthening sunrise the next day'
This sounds to me, a slogan if nice to write, yet
not patently accurate and can even be interpreted
as lowering the value of
the intelligence
that knows a thing or two about 'rising.'

By the way,
I checked this statement at twilight
the sunset was even observed
in "Cogan Marina" in Oslo.

And the sunrise the following morning amounted to an
incline that I trod and rose from a flat, slightly elevated
footpath that can be climbed by foot and reach a level
slightly higher by a few centimeters between each stair.

Secondly, there is no necessity for the sunset I
feel it covering itself every evening between my breasts
beyond the western horizon
watching from within the earth while I am
in the east.

So it is true, some phenomena occur with the rising of the
sun such as, as we rise higher, the atmosphere is thinner at a
height of a few hundred meters and then it dissipates into
space and there are also those who believe that the sun's red
color at sunset is explained by the sun passing in the evening
over hell and in the morning at sunrise over the roses of
paradise and this is indeed a nice allegory.
– but –

In order to remain sane
immediately after sunset I adopt the time between the suns –
time between day
and night
that ends with the stars' coming out
When I rise for the morning prayer and recite the blessing "I
thank you in front of you," opposite a hazy
mirror

Observing every wheel of the sun under the line
of view is a creation that many
have knowledge of

It is known that in the Jewish halacha (ritual law) that the
time of the sunset determines the timeline for various
commandments, such as the mincha afternoon prayer,
or when the Sabbath
commences

For me? It's just sunset.

About the Poet:

Tali Cohen Shabtai, was born in Jerusalem, Israel, and is an international Poet whose works have been translated into many languages. She is the author of three bilingual volumes of Poetry, "Purple Diluted in a Black's Thick" (2007), "Protest" (2012), and "Nine Years from You" (2018). A fourth volume is forthcoming in 2021.
Facebook ID: @Tali Cohen Shabtai

Angel Njoki Chege

(Kenya)

Killing to Live

(Human Organs Trafficking)

In an attempt to bring back their debilitated beloved,
Who may never make it to life,
Deadly stuck in a coma,
Due to lack of
kidney,
melted with damn smoking leisure,
Lost sight,
from prohibited pombe,
Hurtful
heart burning like evil fire.
The Raging Inferno so unbearable,
As flashback fills me mind,
About that day,
Putrescine filled the compound,
In neighboring road,
Accident was first guess,
Mamayoh!!! It wasn't,
ambiguous facial expression,
Stared at me,
Maybe of fear, but the trauma was a guarantee,
Corpse without a belly skin,
Below belt content exposed,
Looking like some sorts of ropes,
collapsed,
Left an orphan,
Baby of a single mother,
Now sleeping in the graveyard,
Without her kidney, heart, eyes, liver, and cervical bones,
They are alive.
In the bodies of inhumane billionaires.
Only the eyes are in the refrigerator,

Waiting for the master's son,
Who has cancer of the eye?
Inhumane, barbaric, evil, wicked,
To kill, To live.

About the Poet:

Angel Njoki Chege is an open-minded student. She is pursuing an undergraduate degree in pharmacy. She loves reading literature and is in love with words. This is her first published work. You can follow Angel on Instagram @angelchegePoetry

Aleksandra Vujisić

(Podgorica, Montenegro)

Back To The Rocks

The waves are rushing to the rocks,
breaking themselves like parts
of a beautiful kaleidoscope
and although the stones never lose,
the waves never stop.

My heart is calling you from the shore,
never too sure if it receives your calls–
breaking itself on the rocks,
the tide rises, the tide falls.

The waves are rushing to the rocks,
and I could never imagine
it could be any other way,
just like I could not stop
searching for you on the horizon,
despite what the sea gods say.

My eyes are searching for
clouds but they only find
the rocks – nature's walls,
and although my heart is not
a good sailor it continues –
the tide rises, the tide falls.

About the Poet:
Aleksandra Lekić Vujisić was born in Podgorica, Montenegro in 1979. She is a professor of English language and literature, and a passionate writer of prose and Poetry for children and grown-ups. She participated in Poetry festivals across Europe, and her work won prizes and acknowledgments in Montenegro and worldwide. Aleksandra writes in her native language and English, and her stories and Poetry have been published several times and translated into Italian, Spanish, and Chinese language.

Gordana Karakashevska

(Skopje, North Macedonia)

My Love For You Is Everlasting

I leave my ghosts
to be with you, darling
I come, reach the destination
and you don't know
I have an ache,
This pain is my own.
I come to be with you.
Hug me, quickly
Give me a little love, my lover.
I let fright and the suffering far behind me.
I love you foolishly!
I`m crazy about you!
My love for you is everlasting.

About the Poet:
Gordana Karakashevska writes poems and short stories in Macedonian, Italian, Serbian, and English. Her poems have been translated into other languages and published in domestic and international online groups, magazines as well as anthologies. A book of short stories *"Signor Giordano and the thoughts about ..."*, a book of Poetry *"Broken Poet and Other Poems"* and a novel *"Nudity"* came out in April / May 2021.
Instagram Handle: @anakarakash

Edith Abdon

(Quezon, Philippines)

A Letter To Myself

Dear Woman,
I hope you're well
I know you were crying yesterday
Because of a broken heart
I hope the wound heals soon
Though I know it's not easy
And the night would be so long.

I hope you're well
I know today you still got up early
Like nothing happened last night
You still faced the mirror
And fixed yourself
You cleared the traces of grief with pride.

I hope you're well
I know you've sensed those judging looks
As you entered that office
With your high-heeled shoes and graceful moves
And a smile so genuine
Who can ever tell you got the blues?

I hope you're still doing well
I know it's been a long day
And the challenges were tough
But you aced it all like an armored warrior
You came back home with flying colors
Though you fought with a heavy heart.
But I know you're well
Though your heart is still broken

And the night would still be long
Like the sun you'll still get up in the morning
To pick up those shattered pieces
And make them whole again.

Dear Woman,
You are a true beauty
In all its sense
Rise up and keep going
Shine like the sun
Each and every morning.

About the Poet:
Edith Abdon was born and raised in the small town of Candelaria in Quezon Province, Philippines. She works from home as a Virtual Admin Assistant. In her spare time, she loved writing poems, short stories, and essays.
LinkedIn ID: @Edith Abdon

Pertunia Pole

(Pretoria, South Africa)

Our Love Is Home

I had opened up my heart like a doorway for you to peek inside
Although there was an emptiness that lingered where my heartbeat once upon a time
Although my soul was darker than my midnight black hair
Although everything I touched turned to ash
You swore to brighten my already dull eyes and revive my soul with just a touch of love
You promised our love was purer than what I had caged up in my chest and used to sound so much like a heart
I told you loving me was like walking on a tightrope with no safety net
You tried to brighten up my life with the stars that shined through your eyes
I let you pull me in slowly, your eyes resembling constellations of the stars, so beautiful yet so far away
We tried to paint our love different shades of red, blue, yellow, white, anything to get rid of the darkness that never left my bare soul
But we can't change what's existed for so long
You cannot build a home inside a home
You really tried to brighten up my life but even a candle goes out in the wind
I'm sorry you got lost in the darkness I had conjured up to protect myself
I'm sorry you got lost in the maze of the walls I built to protect myself
When I told you I was too far from saving
When I told you the darkness had now become a part of me
You said you had a light in you to fight the darkness, to fight me

I'm sorry I put out your burning candle and took the only light you had left
And now all your colors have faded leaving you to harbor darkness like me
I'm sorry I do not have better words to say, perhaps if I could be stronger someday I'll find you
Maybe this time it could be my turn to save you
Maybe we can build our own darkness we'll call home
Our little space of drowning daily
Nobody ever said love had to make sense anyway.

About the Poet:
Pertunia Pole is a BIS Information Science graduate from the University of Pretoria in South Africa who started writing as a hobby to express herself. She has a blog titled "Why is the earth round? We should question these things" which she created as a platform to post some of her work. For her, writing has always been about connecting with others and telling one's story.
Instagram Handle: @bella_donna3263

Sachini Sooriyabandara

(Colombo, Sri Lanka)

Restricted Life

Make time because it's your life,
Lots of thoughts to win the world but ends with no one knowing you died.
Make time to be the one you like,
The journey is harder when you deal with others' likes and dislikes.
In life, you will have to fight,
Life will never give you roses without the hurting thorns for the first time.
It can be pain with a little wound that
leaves a scar on you.
But in the end, it's you who learn with time.

How old are you and how long will you stay?
Do you have an answer? No, I would say.
Out of the time you have spent so far, how much have you given for yourself?
If none is your answer just run as fast as you can!
Stop, hold and think for a while—
Have you been fair to you at any time?
How much you commit to others in life
But not kept a moment just for yourself?
Then come Mother's and Father's wishes on time—
Someone else too will try as long as you stay shy.
When is the number for you, in the waiting list so full?
Will you be able to make your wish come true?
Oh dear, how long will you wait in life?

About the Poet:
Sachini Sooriyabandara is a young Poet from Sri Lanka. She loves penning down in both English and Sinhala. She is also looking forward to write in other languages and reach the world through the universal language of Poetry.

Lis Lovén

(Växjö, Sweden)

To My Lady Of Adoration…

Although Lady Dame, you are highborn – and
You erased my knowledge in stubborn ways…
That´s how I ran off with a criminal band…
Although my odd crime was the sun´s own rays…

You triggered my searching for wisdom here!
But you know very well it cannot sell…
So always and ever are knowledge´s fear!
That´s what I say, and no more I can tell…

So I try to be humble, yet I´m rude…
Cause I figured out nothing in your school!
But why, tell me why is the verse my food…
Oh, could it be that I am a fool?

About the Poet:

Lis Lovén is in her 60s and has been writing Poetry since the age of 15. She lives in the very south of Sweden and has been studying European literature, art, history, cultural sociology. She began to study at Plymouth University in Media Arts. She lives in an area of Växjö with the refugeés, and will soon publish her own sonnets.

Viola Le Compte

(Helsingborg, Sweden)

My Melody

Otherworldly
You come to me
My melody

Linger softly,
Sing to me
So, I can hear

Just the words you suggest
For your verse to get undressed

The right chords to express
All the stories you possess

From a dream,
You came to me
My melody

While I was sleeping
You whispered
Into my ear

Here I am
Write me down
I won't return
So, wake up now

Before I slip
Away like sand
From your grasping
Empty hands

About the Poet:
Viola Le Compte is a classically trained bassist turned singer-songwriter from Belgium. She has recorded and released two albums with original songs ("Love is love", 2017, and "Home", 2020), and one Christmas EP ("Let your heart be light", 2021). She is inspired by life, love, art, nature, and stories. Viola currently lives and works in Sweden.
Instagram Handle: @violalecompte

Monica Buxton

(Somerset, United Kingdom)

The Beauty of Living

I drift into a world of music that gently brushes my ear with tender murmurings, whispering sweet love missives on the string of an angel's harp.

I feel the warmth of the sun and smell the green pastures while the ripples of a brook fill my heart with natural glorious endowments which all of nature's inhabitants of this world have the pleasure to delight in so the music plays on, and on through the song of a bird or an angel's harp, or the music that comes from the soul, and can be sung to please so much.

The voice when soft and gentle gives a warmth to soften the so often harshness of life.

The voice as an instrument can lift the soul, the heart, remove the pain of thoughts that may need soothing.

All instruments have their place either in an orchestra or solo. It doesn't matter where you are in the world, there can always be music, song, and dance. We can fill our hearts and minds with so much joy if we can fight the demons that sometimes haunt or drift in unexpectedly as if to say I'm a reminder that to really enjoy these precious moments, we have to have faced or struggled at times to know how it is to overcome all obstacles and feel the thrill of being alive. Oh WOW! We're alive, what an amazing journey to be on!! It moves the heart to sing and to listen to nature's music of life.

About the Poet:

Monica Buxton is an experienced Poet with a demonstrated history of working in the arts and crafts industry. She is skilled in photography and computers. She has graduated from Holden House private. You can follow Monica on LinkedIn @Monica Buxton

Natasha Shrimpton

(Liverpool, United Kingdom)

The Eyes Do Not See...

I sit on the rocks and look out at the ocean
I see nothing but water for miles
Life is not here, I don't see it
But because I don't see it, it does not mean it's not there.
It's hidden beneath the waves
There is life under the waves the eye will not see
I can walk to the water and listen but nothing can I hear
Nothing I can see
I put my hand in the water and feel it swish by
I look down at my stomach and put my hand gently on it.
I can't see you, hear you or feel you
That does not mean you are not there
You have the potential to grow until you leave the waves but that was not intended
So now I wait lost, lonely and isolated
I wait for nature to take its course
They couldn't see, feel or hear you but I knew you were there
I sit on the rocks looking out at the ocean
I see nothing but water for miles
I can't see you doesn't mean you are not there
In my heart, I felt you
I have seen you in my mind
The people on the rocks looking at the ocean see nothing but water for miles.

About the Poet:

Natasha Shrimpton is a mother of three beautiful children. She has recently finished her studies in therapeutic counselling. Natasha writes to express her feelings and emotions that are sometimes too hard to voice.

Tracey Ramsden

(Dover, Kent, United Kingdom)

Rise Of The Dragon

It is the 49th year of my life
And I am still surprised by the ferocious dragon
That lies within me.
It is 21 years since he died.
I can never forget
But don't always remember.

How can I not remember
The giver of my life?
Why do I choose to forget
The rise of the fiery dragon
That passed to me when he died,
And now lies dormant within me?

It fools me. It tricks me.
Doesn't want me to remember,
Tells me it also died
With his life.
And so it sleeps.
The dragon sleeps.
But I don't forget.

I can't forget
The burning rage haunts me.
Smoldering deep in my belly,
The dragon
taunts me to remember
my early life.
That time until he died.

But has it died?

Can I forget
Its skulking presence in my life?
It's a legacy of burns to me
A scorching memory to remember –
The branding of my dragon.

It spread its wings, the dragon
Rose within him and he died
Not trying to expel its rage, but to remember,
So in turn, I may forget
That dragon lurking deep inside me
Hiding in the corners of my life.

And there the dragon lies while I forget
It has not died.
Ready to rise, it languishes inside me,
Makes me remember, just as he did,
how fire rules my life.

About the Poet:
Tracey Ramsden is a Creative and Professional Writing undergraduate at Canterbury Christchurch University. She has a particular interest in the paranormal, historical fiction, and Victorian horror. As a working mother, Tracey is also an expert in tearing her hair out while juggling many different lives, a reality she likes to explore in her writing.
Instagram Handle: @tracey_ramsden

Brenda Arledge

(Washington Court House, Ohio, United States)

Harboring Anguish

Like a sword, his actions cut like glass
Slashing her heart into pieces,
The pain deep like the bottom of a well
Broken beyond repair.

She locks herself behind closed doors
Harboring the anguish,
Using her fingers to mute the volume on her phone.

Restless torment steady in her veins,
Lost in a maze with no way out,
Seeking peace, but finding nightmares.

About the Poet:

Brenda Arledge is a Poet from the United States. She believes Poetry is the turmoil of one's emotion that comforts the soul and connects people together. Her belief statement: "Make the Most Out of Life".

Instagram Handle: @brendajarledge

Candace Owens

(Lexington Kentucky USA)

Power Inside

People have a power deep inside that they do not know they have.
They think it is bad, but it is on their good behalf.
This power has the power of making dreams come true.
This power lies within every one of you.
Some people find this power is hard to find.
This power can become stronger than the human mind.
It lies beneath your clothes and your hair.
It helps you choose what you are going to wear.
It sometimes feels like a burden that we wish not to bear.
This power is stronger than the human heart.
Without this power, we can become angry and it can tear the soul apart.
You may not know what power I am trying to say, others of you already have this power and use it every day.
I will give you a few more clues, after this it is up to you!
This power is in all people no matter what we do.
Let me guess you think this power is in our mind or in a book?
You are thinking so hard, but have you truly stopped thinking and looked?
This power helps you make decisions in everything you do.
This power helps you solve problems without stressing and life starts to feel like a dream come true.
I will share this power so read this well, as this power is not something that is ever for sale!
This power is being confident in everything you say and do.
The power to love yourself even if you make mistakes will make you feel inspired and brand new.
So, will you activate the power and change your life view?

About the Poet:
Candace Owens has worked at the University of Kentucky in Lexington Kentucky for seventeen years in the healthcare setting. She has been through many challenges but always managed to succeed. Candace had 9 abdominal surgeries; in one she almost died on the operating table in 2016. She is a single mom to an awesome little boy who saved her. She loves writing Poetry and her goal is to spread happiness and hope to the ones who need it. She has successfully created her own Poetry website and is determined to help awaken the world to the beauty in words and how creativity heals. You can follow Candace on Instagram @Poetrypioneer

Christina Isobel

(Sebastopol, California, United States)

A Winter's Journey Into Night

Sky
A flat blackness
Like the back of a mirror
Reflecting me back
To inside myself
It's simple—
I am
Seeing back
Through the mirror
Up to stars
Oh, God!
I am them
I come from them
I am—
My neck hurts
From straining
Craning to see
Oh, honey
Let go
Make love
To those endless points of
Light
I am starlight
Falling
To earth
Being
Born
Again

About the Poet:
Christina Isobel is a Poet, lyricist, and playwright. She created & produced Poetry/dance concerts with Robert Bly. She co-founded a theatre, wrote and co-designed the Poetry/art book, Everyday Mermaid with other artists & published it.
Instagram Handle: @christinaisobel

Heidi Behr

(Orlando, Florida, USA)

Why I Sing Loud At Funerals

At my dad's funeral
all I wanted to do was to sing out loud.

He sure did love it when we sang loud at
church.

Singing is praying twice
we were always told.

So much of the mass can be sung,
so much of it lives in our hearts.

The songs were in my heart as usual,
but got caught in my throat that day.

The crooked hallelujahs
made more tears come to my eyes.

I just wanted to sing for my dad,
even as my heart was breaking.

This is why I sing loudly at funerals now,
I lend my voice to those who can't,
to those who someday want to sing again.

About the Poet:
Heidi Behr is a Psychological and Spiritual Well-Being Expert, Self-empowerment Author, Licensed Therapist, Speaker, Workshop & Retreat leader, EFT-Tapping Expert, Yoga and Happiness Practitioner. You can follow Heidi on Instagram @HeidiBehrLCSW

Mary Beth Kaplan

(Chesterton, USA)

Realistic Sound

Flipping inside out
Holding steadfast
to the base.

Looking up
through the canopy
Light darts
spinning arrows
spiral fest
feeding my aura
Nourishing my
crown
Swelling golden
spine.

Stacking my
bones
straight
Clicking them
together
Shifting.

Like puzzle pieces
click, click, clicked.

Connected and
collected
within
the roots wrapped
warmly
safely sublime
hug suspended.

Held.

Looking up
sprinkles of water
shower each feature
Like falling leaves
ready for sleep
Drifting.

I am safe.
Eyes closed.
Supported and
straight and
crooked and
Real.

I am expressed.
Rested.
The teacher
gently speaks.

Like the
sparrow
calls from
the highest
perch.
Invested.

The naad served
gifted
forever
automatically
now and forever
heard
Lifted.

About the Poet:

Mary Beth Kaplan lives in Northern Indiana with her husband and three beautiful kids. She is a small shop proprietor, an amateur writer and artist. She loves listening to The Beatles, gardening and anything vintage.

Instagram Handle: @the_paperbackmama

Mary Christine Parks

(Wilmington, NC USA)

Purrrr

I've grown into a kitten
From a lioness
Shed my rough coat
For the softest fluff
Allowed the caresses
Of safe, adoring hands

I've released my pride
Embraced play
Let go
My NO
For the curiosity of
M A Y B E

I've retracted my claws
Paused
To listen
Be led
Banishing the Alpha
To find right size

I roar less
Preferring to purr
Spontaneous and free
Unencumbered
I've grown into a kitten
From a lioness

About the Poet:
A creative at heart, Mary Christine can be found most days writing, sculpting, gardening, or playing with her three kids. That is when she is not working as a psychotherapist specializing in trauma and addiction or teaching yoga or meditation. Her work, love of life, and fascination with the Earth and its inhabitants imbues her writing with the full spectrum of human emotion.
Instagram Handle: @mary.christine.parks

Aarti Bansal

(Faridabad, India)

I Look For Inspiration In The Gust Of Wind

In city crowds and empty fields,
Turning to things and back where it begins
I look up to the soaring clouds and barren trees.

I wonder where it could be,
In soulful cries or twisted lies.
In shattered illusions that are dug through the debris,
Leaping high maybe in those tides.

Obsessively, incessantly I yearn to find,
I look in the groaning glaciers and endless white.
With the unusual peace that turns my mind,
Some isolated memory fragments come alive.

The mirror ruminates my deepest scar.
Wearing it with pride,
I stumble upon inspiration
that is shimmering in the dark.

About the Poet:
Aarti bansal is the muse in the ink, her words rebel in the dark. A mother to two, she loves scribbling poems.
Instagram Handle: @musings_ink

Anuja Churi

(Boisar, India)

Adoption

Hey, I picked up parents last night!
One gets cherry red when she cries,
The other seems vampire white
They'll want to pass on their warmth
I'll clench my fist tight
How can they intrude now,
I'm all blaze and uptight,
I can't mellow down now,
I have yearned all this while
Let them try their core
I'll hold my guard all my might
Why does God answer in the Sun
When you've yelled all over the night?
Why would you grip onto the dreary dream?
When the truth will set it all right?

About the Poet:

Anuja Churi is an enthusiastic straight edge who outwardly believes in ethics, morals, and ethos and inherently seeks setting it all right! She adores intellectual conversations and in-depth cogitations over politics, language, socio-cultural issues, and otherworldly concerns. She likes to delve deep into the matters of ingenuity, oration, and eloquence. You can follow Anuja on Twitter @coshstruck

Chaithra MJ

(Bangalore, India)

Imagine, If You Will

Imagine, if you will
That you've been imprisoned for the rest of your life
In solitary, in a dark room with a small window
The only passage of light inside a dark territory

Your life is ruled by schedules now
Your meals, your sleep, your recess
A bell becomes your alarm clock
Siren, your lullaby
Chaos and emptiness blurring the lines of sanity

All you need is a moment of silence
In this ever haunting mayhem
Commotion, your constant companion
Freedom, a distant dream
Absolution, your only hope

Despair crawling into your skin
Choked by misery, poisoned by isolation
Day by day, moment by moment
Feeling the wrath in its full glory
Desperately waiting for the Day of Atonement

Liberation is an oasis in the desert of imprisonment
The privilege of choice, a myth
Eternity smirking with mockery
Irony frolicking with 'FREE'dom

Now snap back to reality
Sink into the realization
You are free
You are free

You are free to choose
To be the author of your own story
To be the captain of your own journey
To be the artist of your own canvas

You are bestowed with a precious gift
A prized possession to be treasured
The power of choice
The power to do, have or be anything and everything

Freedom is a privilege available to all but realized by few

Why live a life of mental confinement when you're exempted?
Why live a life of shackles when you can break free?
Why live the life of a caged bird when you can soar high?

About the Poet:
Chaithra MJ is a Content writer from Bangalore. She believes writing is a form of therapy to express oneself truly. Being a bibliophile from a young age, she grew up with books as her friends and writing as her muse.
LinkedIn Id: @Chaithra MJ

Chaitra Ramalingegowda

(Bangalore, India)

Set The Words Free

If I could write I'd set all the words free,
Free to follow you,
To tell you all the
Wonder and secrets
Of life and love and solitude,
Of all that's mysterious,
Of wisdom that comes with experience.

If I could write I'd set all the words free,
Free to hug you
And keep you warm at night,
Shield you from the dark,
When you feel cold and alone,
When you're not you,
When loneliness haunts you.

If I could write I'd set all the words free,
Free to weave your dreams
Of tomorrow and all the days after,
With hope stitched in there
That they come true
One day – soon,
Because words are all I have.

About the Poet:
Chaitra Ramalingegowda fell in love with storytelling long before she knew what it was. She loves well-written stories, writing with passion, baking lip-smacking-finger-licking chocolate cakes, watching engaging movies, and home-cooked food. A true work-in-progress, she's a believer in JRR Tolkien's quote, 'not all those who wander are lost.' Instagram Handle: @chaitra.ramalingegowda

Damayanti Bhadra

(Kolkata, India)

We Grew Up

From nerds to teens, we grew up,
From going to school to college, we grew up,
From having chocolates to cigarettes, we grew up,
From laughing out loud at jokes
To holding each other tightly under the midnight moon, we grew up.

From solving algebras to solving us, we grew up,
From too many colors to only black, we grew up,
From fighting with each other to fighting for us, we grew up,
From crying out loud to hiding tears on each other's shoulders, we grew up.

From spreading colors on each other
to getting drenched in the rains, we grew up.

From growing up together to going apart, we grew up.

About the Poet:
Damayanti Bhadra is a Philosophy honors student at the Presidency University. She is an amateur photographer and a book lover.
Instagram Handle: @bhadra_shots

Neha Agarwal

(Kolkata, India)

Dream of You

I dreamt of you last night
I was with you under the moonlight
My eyes were entranced by your love
My heart was drifted by your presence
The togetherness was enchanting
I wanted to melt in your arms
And hold you for eternity
It was a bewitching dream
I was stitching myself with you
The daylight soon cuddled me
I woke up realizing it was a silent reverie

About the Poet:
Neha Agarwal is a professional Makeup artist and a designer cake specialist who loves scribbling poems when she is not working. One of her poems has got published before in an international magazine.
Instagram Handle: @glamandglow_makcover

Nikita Munshi Aggarwal

(Mumbai, India)

On the Run

They say to run away, to escape
Is cowardly.
But maybe, some people are built that way.

I did it when I was ten and had stage fright
I did it when I was thirteen, to avoid failing
a math test,
I did it when I was sixteen, to hide the lone
red zit on my face.

I did it when I was twenty-four, to save myself
From committing to a relationship.

I've been a runner all my life,
It's the only life I know.

But something in me rings differently now.

I don't want to win the race anymore,
I don't want to be the sprinter,
I want to be a marathoner.
So maybe, this time I won't escape.

I'll be the last one standing,
With open arms, waiting for you.
And once I have you, I won't need to run away
For we'll have each other to escape into.

About the Poet:

Nikita Munshi Aggarwal is a Mumbai-based Poet and writer. She launched her debut Poetry book "Soft Glimmers & Shining Stars" in 2021. Previously, she has worked as a management consultant, spending 5 years in the strategy and risk space. Nikita has an appetite for the extraordinary and has traveled to 22 countries in 29 years. You can follow Nikita on Instagram @niki.munshi

Pragati Adbol

(Navi Mumbai, India)

Deserted Island

Deserted Island is the place where I wish to be.
As I look at the horizon, I ponder whether the sky came first or the sea.

Along with the rhythmic waves, I retrieve my peace again!
As I travel through the blue ocean, I feel happy about the expedition.

I found solace in this solitude, which filled my heart with gratitude.
As I feel thankful and blessed, I know that my happiness will never fade.

It's a journey of life balancing pleasure and pain.
As it rejuvenates my body, mind, and soul I wish to visit this deserted island once again.

About the Poet:

Pragati Adbol is a Poet, co-author, and freelance management consultant. She has a decade of experience in management consultancy and feels that motivation is required daily. She writes about her passions and thoughts. Her Poem "The sound of silence" and others have been published in international magazines.
Instagram Handle: @Pragati_Adbol

Pragya Maheshwari

(Nagpur, India)

Life Is A Loop

Born with loud outcry gender naming girl
Said to be the angel but she keeps coloring others' home
Has a dream to touch the sky but she has to pull down for a guy!
Love and care are said to be a must in her character but she keeps fighting to stand in a line of the Toppers
Understanding her is easy but the world tries not to understand her
She is taught to be a perfectionist but expected to accept other's faults
"Change and Dynamic" should be her hold but
landed "adjusting and compromising" on the role
She believes to be free and bold but judgment is always the way of her.
She wants to wear shirts and dresses but is desired to be in drapes of the loom
To be wrapped for!
Remember Life is a Loop.
She is strong to create a new life.
Though the one who will be born from her womb with a loud cry is often expected to be a boy
They say the world has changed but the mentality remains the same!

About the Poet:

Pragya Maheshwari hails from the city of oranges, Nagpur. She is a digital marketer and content writer, pursuing career counseling. Poetry writing is her hobby.

Shweta Rastogi

(Mumbai, India)

Why Do You Wail O Heart?

Behold! This heart is plagued, appalled, and bruised!
Masquerading, they sheathe the trials and triumphs of my creed,
Unsung are the deeds and throttled my excruciating need,
Incessantly and viciously, I'm slandered and abused.
Ablaze with indignation, their jaundiced eyes leave me indisposed.
For ages, this talent, hankering for incentives, lies as a latent seed.
Its potency is restrained and decreed; it wails wanting some heed.
O! It laments in agony, now this torment can't be eternally endured.

He sent you onstage with a stout flair and hoards of hopes,
Persevere and perform, the undaunted He's your admirer and spectator.
Crib not, cry not, resent further not as your time is too short.
Envisioning your mantle reaching the pinnacle,
His blessings on you constantly He bestows.
With Him beside, nothing exists that you can't devour and resist.
Do you still fancy more?
Lest sit on the grave repenting,
Escorted by grit with this too you could've fought.

About the Poet:

Shweta Rastogi is an educator, artist, and author. She writes motivational and spiritual articles and poems, and stories on the lives of women from different strata. The title of the LITERARY COLONEL has been conferred upon her for her contribution in the field of Literature.

Sneha Sonkar

(Kolkata, India)

Shrill Dark Music

Shrill dark music is all I heard standing at the threshold of a forest, which I can hardly hear now.

Devoid of hefty trees that were once its pride.

Rivers once glistened by the sunrays and the moonlight have now become dark.

Pollution and deforestation have taken their toll on the forest, sucking their verdure out of them.

The sky cried seeing the degraded forest, which was once lush green.

And the animals?
They sighed in melancholy for their home was no longer the same.

The cool breeze no more caressed their skin like they used to, And the tree shades that once covered their heads, protecting them from the scorching sun and torrent rain, hardly gave them a home-like feeling now.

It all changed immensely and this is their heart-wrenching story.

About the Poet:
Sneha Sonkar is a B.Sc student at St. Xavier's College, Kolkata. She loves sketching and penning down Poetry when she is not studying.

Sunandita Mukherjee

(Durgapur, India)

Trapped

I could feel drops of fear running down my cheeks
I was sobbing, feeling lonely
Something aching in my heart sorely
For the knife of doubts stabbed me slowly

Knotting up in my veins
Something tightening in my brain
This pain was not something my eyes could hide
In front of the one, my trust had lied

Kneeling, trying to be free
A war-torn world was all I could see
Then I heard a voice from within
As if trying to persuade me to win

The night, cold and dark
surrounded me
The twinkling stars
reflected on the blood underneath

My dull brown scars
Reminded me of my caged presence
My hands in this cage still drew blood
It was only freedom that I searched
I felt that voice inside me again
And the teardrops my eyes had shed
This time with more desire to be free
I break open this cage of vulnerability
Listening to words
That is helping to be me

About the Poet:
Sunandita Mukherjee is a high school student from Durgapur. She loves painting, dancing, and penning down Poetry. When she is free, she loves cooking exotic cuisine and reading books. Instagram Handle: @sunandita_m

Dear Readers,

Here we come to the end of an incredible journey! Thank you for taking the time to read through the pieces by 40 women poets around the world!

If you have enjoyed this book and have a minute to spare, we would really appreciate a short review on the page or site where you bought this book.

Please help spread the word about our book.

With profound gratitude,
Poets,
Expressions from the Heart

www.ingramcontent.com/pod-product-compliance
Lightning Source LLC
LaVergne TN
LVHW091230150826
845673LV00003B/1084

* 9 7 8 9 3 9 0 5 6 7 3 0 0 *